# BLAZE AND THE
# LOST QUARRY

## More Billy and Blaze Books
## by C. W. Anderson

# BLAZE AND THE LOST QUARRY

Story and Pictures by C. W. ANDERSON

Aladdin Paperbacks

Revised Cover Edition, 2000
Aladdin Paperbacks
An imprint of Simon & Schuster
Children's Publishing Division
1230 Avenue of the Americas
New York, NY 10020
First Aladdin Paperbacks edition 1991
Printed in the United States of America
10   9   8   7

Library of Congress Cataloging-in-Publication Data
Anderson, C. W. (Clarence William), date.
Blaze and the lost quarry: Billy and Blaze find the way story and pictures /
by C. W. Anderson. — 1st Aladdin Books ed.
p.      cm.
Summary: Billy and his pony Blaze discover the way to an abandoned quarry where they perform a
brave deed.
ISBN 0-689-71775-X
[1. Ponies—Fiction.]    I. Title.
PZ7.A524Blbl   1994
[E]—dc20
93-10721

To Francis Coolidge
and his pony, Cranberry

Billy was a boy who had a pony
with four white feet and a wide white
stripe on his face. This is called
a "blaze," so Billy named his
pony Blaze. Billy loved Blaze very
much and took the best care of him.

They went for long rides through the woods. Some of the roads were forgotten and nobody ever used them. Billy loved to explore, and Blaze seemed to like it too. They saw many birds and rabbits and squirrels.

One day Billy and Blaze stopped by
a little house. An old man sat out
in the sun. He was very friendly
and asked Billy where he rode. "Have
you ever seen the old quarry?" he
asked. "They call it the lost quarry
now because nobody seems to know
where it is."

The old man went on: "I knew it well as a boy, but I am too old and crippled to go there and show you the way. Look for a small road to the left with deep ruts made by oxcarts. Then when you come to Wolf Rock you will know you are on the right road."

Billy found the road. It was just as
the old man had told him, with deep
tracks that the oxcarts had made
long ago. Billy was very excited.
Soon he would see the quarry he had
heard so much about.

The road was overgrown, and Billy had to bend low to get under the trees and vines. He could see that it was many, many years since this road had been used.

Then they came to a place so overgrown
with hanging vines that Blaze could not
get through. Blaze stood quietly while
Billy took out his pocket knife and
cut away the vines. Then they went on.

After riding a long way they came to a large rock beside the road. On it were cut the words WOLF ROCK. Billy had often heard the story of how a man had once climbed up on this rock when attacked by wolves. He had held them off with a club until daylight, when they went away, as wolves do.

Farther on Billy saw a strange piece of stone beside the road. There were deep marks cut into it. Now he knew he was on the right road, for this stone must have come from the quarry.

They went for quite a way, and then
Billy saw something that made him
pull up short. A large dead tree
had fallen across the road. It was
a big tree, but he knew Blaze was
a good jumper. Billy would not turn
back now, for he knew they were near
the lost quarry.

He turned Blaze around to get a start
and then called, "Come on, Blaze."
It seemed like flying as they sailed
over the tree in a big leap. Blaze
galloped along shaking his head.
He liked jumping and excitement.

Then around a turn in the road
they came to a tumbledown house.
Some of the men who worked in the
quarry must have lived here long,
long ago.

Farther on Billy saw a smooth stone
beside the road. It looked strange,
so he got off his pony for a careful
look. 1884, he read. He knew this
came from the quarry. He must be
very close now.

And suddenly there it was! It was
bigger than Billy had thought, with
high walls and deep, clear water.
What a wonderful place!

He heard a dog barking, and then he saw a red fox running along the very top of the high wall. After him came a brown-and-white dog running as hard as he could.

Suddenly the dog slipped. He scrambled hard to keep from falling, but he could not hold on, and down he came.

The dog hit the water with a splash, but he came up quickly and started swimming. Billy called to him, for he knew the dog could never get up those steep walls. The dog began swimming toward Billy.

Billy lay down and reached as far as he could. He soon got hold of the dog's paws and pulled him out of the water.

Billy wiped him as dry as he could
with his handkerchief. He saw that
the dog had no collar. "You must
be lost," said Billy. "If no one
claims you, then you can be my dog.
Would you like that?" The dog
licked Billy's hands and wagged
his tail happily.

As they started for home the dog went
along proudly. He liked to belong
to somebody. It had been an exciting
day. Billy had found the lost quarry
and also a wonderful place to swim.
And he also had a dog. Blaze went
along gaily, as if he were happy too.